Ivor Cutler

pictures by Claudio Muñoz

TAMBOURINE BOOKS  NEW YORK

Library of Congress Cataloging in Publication Data

Cutler, Ivor. Doris / by Ivor Cutler; illustrated by Claudio Muñoz.
1st U.S. ed. p. cm.
Summary: Doris the hen and Oliver Parrot discover their duets are
not only fun to sing, but lucrative too.
[1. Chickens—Fiction.   2. Parrots—Fiction.   3. Singing—
Fiction.]   I. Muñoz, Claudio, ill.   II. Title.
PZ7.C978Do 1992 [E]—dc20
ISBN 0-688-11939-5
92-5923 CIP AC

Produced by Mandarin
Printed and bound in China.

1 3 5 7 9 10 8 6 4 2

First U.S. edition

To all the girls and boys who can
keep their lips shut tight when
they are being tickled
I.C.

To my son
David
C.M.

Once upon a time there lived a hen called Doris. She weighed the same as twenty apples. Doris had a lovely voice, as sweet as a bird.

Every morning, she scrubbed the floor of an office and sang
a song about a mouse or some sheep.

People passing on their way to work would stop, raise their heads, and listen to her song as it floated out the window onto the sharp air.

On Monday, Wednesday,
and Friday she sang the
mouse song, which went:
There was a wee mouse
That lived in a pancake....

On Tuesday and Thursday she
would sing the sheep song:
Some white, woolly sheep
Are chewing my carrots to bits....

On weekends she stayed home and tended her nest.

Some people liked the mouse song. Some preferred the sheep song. They crowded round the window when their song was on.

Every morning there was such a crush that people were standing on other people's heads to get a bit of room to listen in peace.

Doris's boss, Oliver Parrot, liked making money, so he dragged a wicker basket out from under his desk, stood in the street, and made people pay as they passed.

If they kept walking while they listened, he charged one penny. If they stopped to listen, he charged three pennies, and if they walked very slowly, Oliver Parrot charged them two pennies.

One Thursday morning after she had scrubbed the floor, Doris was singing the sheep song while she dusted the windowsill. She opened the window to give the fuzzy dust cloth a considerable shake, and what did she see! Oliver Parrot charging people pennies for *her* song.

Her cheeks turned dark red and she yelled down, "What are you up to, Oliver Parrot, eh? What are all those pennies in your basket, you sly parrot?"

Oliver Parrot tried to hide the basket behind his back,
but he was clumsy so Doris could still see it. "I'm earning
you a little money for your old age," he smiled weakly.

"Old age!" clucked Doris in fury, "I'm two years old!"
She flew down onto Oliver Parrot's shoulders and started
singing an entirely new song about how young and lovely
she was.

Everybody was thrilled with the new song. They threw lots of money in the basket and went to work singing it, or humming it if they forgot the words.

So Doris gave up dusting and scrubbing, and spent her weekdays perched on Oliver, singing her new song.

They divided up the money. Doris got eight pennies out of every ten. But Oliver wanted half the money, so one morning he started singing along with Doris.

All the people ran away screaming. Oliver's voice sounded like a million flies with sore stomachs.

"Oh, no!" clucked Doris sympathetically. Large tears made their way onto Oliver's breast feathers, leaving dark marks.

"Wa-ah!" wept Oliver, "I was too greedy." And he told Doris why he had sung. Then he started to moan again.

"Hey, do that some more," clucked Doris.

"Do what?" sniffed Oliver.

"More wa-ah," said Doris.

Oliver, looking puzzled, sucked in some breath, then let it out slowly in a long hum.

"That's a beautiful hum you have, Oliver. You hum and I'll sing—but we'd better practice first. Take my ankle."

Doris flapped her wings and they rose high over town. "We are going to my place on Lonely Mountain."

"Hurry up," mumbled Oliver, "my beak is falling off."

They soon arrived. Lonely Mountain was two hundred
feet high. Doris had built a nest in a cleft near the top.

She cracked five new laid eggs, and they sat down to the
freshest omelette Oliver had ever tasted, followed by
fragrant tea from a bush which sprouted by the edge, and
heavy, dark bread smeared with plum and cinnamon jelly.

The rest of the day was spent practicing Oliver's hum. He had a good ear and hummed in deep harmony. The friendly noise matched Doris's light, high cluck exactly.

The following morning they awoke to cries of "Sing to us, Doris!" They peeked over the edge and there, packed into the valley below and halfway up the mountain, was a great crowd in holiday garb, waiting. The crowd pressed closer, silent.

Doris opened her beak and sang as she had never sung. She winked, and Oliver joined in with his rich hum. There was a gasp from the crowd.

When they finished, nobody spoke. Then suddenly, everyone was clapping like a silver storm. The duo had to sing and hum their song eleven times before the crowd was truly satisfied and returned to town with tears in their eyes, leaving behind gifts in a bathtub that lay near the foot of the slope.

When they were gone, Oliver and Doris
found the tub so full of money it couldn't
be seen. There were even jewels and
fruit and a salmon.

"That was nothing!" laughed Oliver.
"Wait till Monday at the office."

"Wait for what?" clucked Doris.

"You know! Lots of money!" said Oliver.

"Don't you enjoy humming?"

"Of course I do!" replied Oliver.

"Well, what do you want more money
for?" she demanded.

Oliver looked in Doris's eyes for a
whole minute. Then he tilted all the
money into a deep hole and threw some
dirt on top of it.

"Come on, Oliver. Breakfast!" clucked
Doris, and they flew up to the nest for
broiled salmon with fruit.

But on Monday, Doris tied the basket to the desk,
just in case.